For my friend Anita and my granddaughter Elena
for their much appreciated work that went into this book
—MD

First published in the United States, Great Britain, Canada, Australia, and New Zealand in 2009
by North-South Books Inc., an imprint of NordSüd Verlag AG, CH-8005 Zürich, Switzerland.
Distributed in the United States by North-South Books Inc., New York 10001.

Library of Congress Cataloging-in-Publication Data is available.
ISBN: 978-0-7358-2227-6 (trade edition).
10 9 8 7 6 5 4 3 2 1
Printed in Belgium

www.northsouth.com

FSC
Mixed Sources
Product group from well-managed
forests and other controlled sources
Cert no. BV-COC-070303
www.fsc.org
© 1996 Forest Stewardship Council

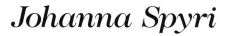

Johanna Spyri

Heidi

illustrated by **Maja Dusíková**

NorthSouth
New York / London

One sunny June morning, a young woman climbed briskly up the steep path that wound its way through the meadows and woods toward the top of the mountain. Holding her hand was a little girl, whose cheeks glowed as if they were on fire. And no wonder, for the child wore three dresses, one over the other, a heavy scarf around her neck, and a straw hat—everything she owned.

The child's name was Heidi, and she had lived with her Aunt Dete ever since she could remember. But now Dete had found a good job in the big city of Frankfurt and Heidi could not go with her. So Dete was taking the little girl to live with her grandfather high on the mountain.

"How can you do such a thing!" said the people in the village below. "Nobody knows what ails the old man up there. Everyone keeps out of his way and is afraid of him."

"What will the child do here?" Grandfather growled.

"That is your business," Dete told him. "Heidi must live with you now." And she set off back down the mountain.

The old man opened the door, and Heidi followed him into a large room. In it were a table and one chair. In the corner was one bed.

"Where shall I sleep, Grandfather?" asked Heidi.

"Wherever you like," he replied.

Heidi climbed a little ladder to the hayloft. There was the sweet smell of fresh hay and a small round window to the sky.

"It is lovely!" she called down. "Come look!"

"I know all about it," said Grandfather.

"I am going to make my bed here," Heidi rushed on. "But you must bring me a sheet, for all beds must have a sheet."

"Well, well," said Grandfather from below, and he went to the cupboard to find a sheet.

The next morning, Heidi was awakened by a loud whistle. Outside was a boy and six goats. "This is Peter," said Grandfather, who was bringing two more goats out of the shed. "And these are Schwänli and Bärli. Peter is taking them up to the pasture. Would you like to go with them?"

"Oh, yes!" cried Heidi, who could think of nothing nicer.

Up on the mountain, Heidi ran through the wildflowers, leaping over rocks as she went. She laughed to watch the goats, who were even better jumpers—big Türk with his powerful horns, nimble Distelfinck, little white Schneehöpli, and the prettiest of all, Grandfather's own Schwänli and Bärli.

For lunch, there was bread and cheese and two bowls of milk from Schwänli—the best lunch in the world, Heidi thought.

Day after day, Heidi and Peter climbed the mountain to the high meadow. Heidi grew rosy-cheeked and strong; she was as happy as the birds.

Months passed and it grew cold. One night, a deep snow fell. After this, the goatherd Peter did not come any more, and Schwänli and Bärli stayed warm in their shed.

Some mornings Grandfather fetched a sled, bundled Heidi up cozily, and off they flew, down the mountainside to Peter's hut. Peter's grandmother was waiting for them. She was blind, and her days were dark; but Heidi's merry tales of Schwänli and Bärli and their adventures on the mountain seemed to light up the room. A joy had come into the grandmother's life, for now she had Heidi to look forward to.

While Heidi and the grandmother visited, Grandfather busied himself with his hammer and tools, patching up the old hut. "He has changed," thought the grandmother, "since Heidi came."

And so the winter passed, and it was summer again, then winter once more, and then again spring. Heidi had never been so happy.

Heidi was now seven, and though she had learned much about the mountain, she could not read. The nearest school was two hours away, and Grandfather would not hear of sending her away. He could no longer imagine the mountain without her.

Then one March day Aunt Dete came again. She had met a rich gentleman in Frankfurt who was looking for a companion for his daughter, Klara, who could not walk. "Heidi will be that companion," said Dete. "Think of the opportunities she will have!"

"I won't go!" said Heidi. But Dete promised, "You can come home whenever you want. And think of the lovely, soft white rolls you can bring the grandmother from Frankfurt."

This idea pleased Heidi, for she knew the grandmother could no longer chew the hard mountain bread.

And so Heidi left the mountain with Aunt Dete.

From that day on, Grandfather's mood darkened as if a light had gone out. He grew more and more silent, his face creased in an unhappy frown.

In Frankfurt, Aunt Dete took Heidi to meet Fräulein Rottenmeier and Klara. Klara's father was away on business much of the time, and when he was away, Fräulein Rottenmeier was in charge.

Klara, who spent each day in a wheelchair, was excited to have a friend. Fräulein Rottenmeier, however, was not at all pleased with Heidi. "This child is far too young!" she complained. "And she cannot even read!" But Klara's father had given orders: Heidi would stay.

Sebastian the butler kept his thoughts to himself. At dinner, when he saw Heidi slip a soft roll into her pocket for the grandmother, he didn't say a word. And when Heidi fell asleep at the table, Sebastian lifted her gently and carried her up to bed.

The next morning, Heidi found herself in a high white bed in a large room. She rushed to the window, but there were no mountains outside, just walls and windows, and more walls and windows, and in the distance a tall church spire.

Klara loved to hear Heidi's stories about Peter and the goats. And Heidi grew very fond of Klara, but still she longed for the mountains. Surely she would be able to see them from the church tower. So one day, while Klara was resting, Heidi set off to find the church.

An old monk kindly showed Heidi the stairs up to the tower. Heidi climbed many, many steps until finally she was at the top. Even here, high above the other buildings, Heidi could not see her mountains. But something else in the tower made Heidi glad that she had come. The monk had a cat, and the cat had kittens.

"Oh, Klara would love these kittens so!" Heidi exclaimed, and the monk was happy to give her some of them.

Fräulein Rottenmeier was horrified. "Sneaky, dirty things!" she cried. "Get those cats out of here right now!"

Luckily for Heidi and Klara, Sebastian liked cats and was pleased to hide the kittens in the attic.

But Heidi could not stay out of trouble. A few days later, Fräulein Rottenmeier discovered all the rolls Heidi had been saving for the grandmother. "Throw this stale bread away!" she ordered.

"No! No!" begged Heidi. "Those rolls are for the grandmother!" And she burst into tears.

"Please don't cry so," said Klara. "I promise I will give you just as many rolls for the grandmother, or even more, when you go home."

One day, Klara's grandmamma came to visit. She brought with her a book full of beautiful pictures for Heidi to read.

"But I can't read," Heidi whispered.

Grandmamma took Heidi's hand. "You can learn to read," she said. "I will teach you. And when you learn, you may have this book to keep."

As the days passed, Grandmamma read stories from the beautiful book. Heidi often turned the pages and watched as Grandmamma showed her the words. By the time Grandmamma left, Heidi herself could read the stories to Klara.

Autumn passed, and winter, and it was spring again. Day after day, the girls read and played together; but Heidi's longing for the mountains did not leave her. How she missed Grandfather and Peter and the grandmother. She lost her appetite and grew thin and pale.

Then strange things began happening in the grand house. Every morning, the front door stood wide open. Though they double locked the door each night, it made no difference. Someone—or something—was opening that door as they slept.

"It's a ghost!" Fräulein Rottenmeier was certain of it. She wrote to Klara's father, who was away on business. He must return to Frankfurt. The house was haunted!

Klara's father came home at once. He did not believe in ghosts, but *something* was going on. Determined to find out what it was, he invited a friend to stay up with him and watch.

At the stroke of midnight, the men heard strange noises and jumped out from their hiding place. Standing in the doorway was a mysterious figure dressed in white. It was Heidi!

Poor Heidi. Each night, in her sleep, she had opened the door and stood there staring, as if she could see her mountains far away.

Klara's father understood. Heidi must be allowed to return to her home in the mountains.

Klara was very upset at the news, but her father was firm. "Heidi's unhappiness is making her ill," he explained. "Only home can bring the roses back to her cheeks." But he promised to take Klara to visit Heidi in Switzerland that summer.

Heidi made the long journey holding in her lap a basket packed by Klara herself. It was full of soft white rolls for the grandmother.

At last Heidi was running up the path toward the little house high on the mountain. There, in the doorway, was Grandfather!

As promised, Klara came in June. She loved the little house and the goats. She loved her days with Heidi and Grandfather.

But Peter was jealous. Heidi was spending all her time with Klara. One day, when they were all in the high meadow, he angrily pushed the wheelchair over a cliff.

"Now I will hold Klara up on one side," Heidi told him. "And you must hold her on the other." Peter did not like this idea at all, but he did it.

"Just stamp right down," Heidi told Klara, and Klara did. Then again. And again. Until suddenly she cried out, "Oh, I can! I can take steps!"

Day by day, Klara's legs grew stronger. And then, suddenly, it was time for her to go home. Her father and Grandmamma came to fetch her. What a surprise they got!

Heidi stood at the edge of the slope and waved until Klara and her family were specks in the distance. She was not going back with them to Frankfurt. Heidi was staying on the mountain—with Peter and the grandmother, with Schwänli and Bärli, with Grandfather. Heidi had come home.